P9-DFO-268

Whose Shoes Are These?

by RON ROY

photographs by

ROSMARIE HAUSHERR

Clarion Books
TICKNOR & FIELDS: A HOUGHTON MIFFLIN COMPANY
New York

This book is for Bobby.
R.R.

Photographer's Note:

The photography in this book is a tribute to my friends and their children. Many of them appear in the photos. Others have lent me shoes or accessories for props, or have helped me with valuable information and contacts. Thank you all very, very much. A warm thank-you also to my editor, Ann Troy, and to Carol Goldenberg and Catherine Stock for their creative book design. Special thanks to: Brenda Allen, Photographer; Caplan's Army & Navy Supplies, St. Johnsbury, Vermont; Catamount Art, St. Johnsbury, Vermont; Corlears School, New York City; Dental Associates, St. Johnsbury, Vermont; Doris Wolff and Robert Convey, Juilliard School of Music, New York City; Goat Works, Washington, New Jersey; Keystone-Press, Zurich, Switzerland; Nazareth Nursery School, New York City; New York City Police Department, Scuba Team; New York Skating Club; Nolin's Shoes, St. Johnsbury, Vermont; Skippy the Clown, New York; The Swiss Institute, New York; Treitel-Gratz Company, Long Island City, New York.

Clarion Books
Ticknor & Fields, a Houghton Mifflin Company
Text copyright © 1988 by Ron Roy
Photographs copyright © 1988 by Rosmarie Hausherr
All rights reserved.
For information about permission to reproduce
selections from this book, write to Permissions,
Houghton Mifflin Company, 2 Park Street, Boston, MA 02108
Printed in the U.S.A.

Library of Congress Cataloging-in-Publication Data
Roy, Ron, 1940-
Whose shoes are these?
Summary: Text and photographs describe the
appearance and function of almost twenty types of shoes,
including work boots, snowshoes, and basketball sneakers.
1. Shoes—Juvenile literature.   [1. Shoes]
I. Hausherr, Rosmarie, ill.   II. Title.
GT2130.R69   1988   391'.413   87-24279
ISBN 0-89919-445-1
H 10 9 8 7 6 5 4 3 2 1

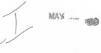

Who wears shoes with
thick, rippled soles?

Runners wear these shoes. Their feet pound the surface of sidewalks and roads as they run. The shoes have thick layers of foam rubber inside to cushion the runners' feet. The rubber soles have ripples so the runners do not slide on slippery places as they run. Running shoes are lightweight.

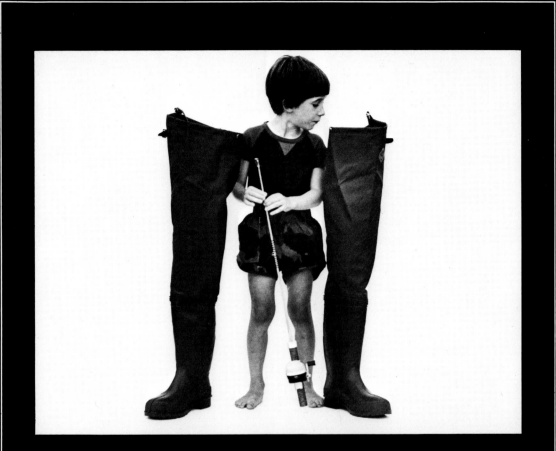

Why are these boots
so tall?

These rubber boots must be tall enough to reach a grown-up's hips or waist. Straps prevent the boots from falling down. The boots are worn by people who wade in deep water. These men work in a fish hatchery, a place where fish eggs hatch. The water there can get very cold. These tall waders keep the workers' feet and legs warm and dry.

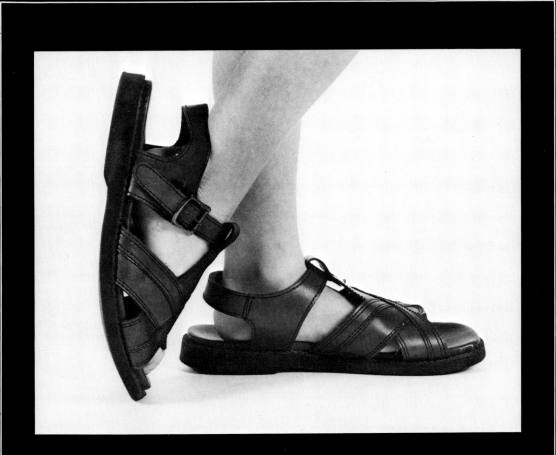

When do you wear open shoes
with straps?

People wear sandals when the weather is warm. Sandals are made so air can pass between the straps and cool the feet. Some sandals have leather straps. Others are made of rubber or plastic. If you wear sandals on the beach, sand can get caught between your foot and the sole of the sandal. If that happens, just lift your foot and shake!

Why does this short boot
have a shiny blade?

This is an ice skate. A strong metal blade is screwed onto the bottom of the leather boot. A skater glides across the ice by balancing on the blades. The boot part of the skate is tightly laced to support the skater's ankle. Do you see those little points on the tip of the blade? Skaters can start or stop fast by digging those points into the ice.

Why is this shoe shaped
like a frog's foot?

Frogs have skin between their toes to help them swim fast. These rubber flippers are shaped like a frog's webbed feet. When a swimmer wearing these flippers moves his feet, the wide rubber pushes the water out of the way and the swimmer shoots forward. This "frogman" works as a diver. He is wearing an oxygen tank so he can breathe underwater.

When is a good time
to wear slippers?

Anytime! Many people wear slippers instead of shoes in the house.
Slippers are easier to put on than shoes, and a lot quieter. They are
usually made of soft, comfortable material so they feel good on
your feet. Some have no backs while others cover the whole foot. Do
you put on cozy slippers when you get up in the morning?

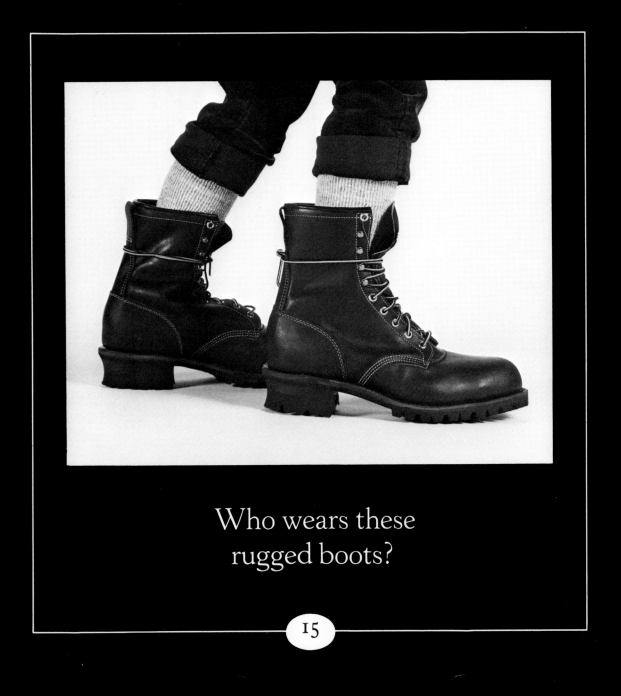

Who wears these
rugged boots?

People who cut timber, climb telephone poles, put up buildings, and work in factories wear these boots. They are made for people who work in dangerous places. A piece of metal inside the boot protects the worker's toes. Strong leather sides give support to the ankles. Those thick soles act like cushions between the worker's feet and hard floors. The ridges prevent the workers from slipping.

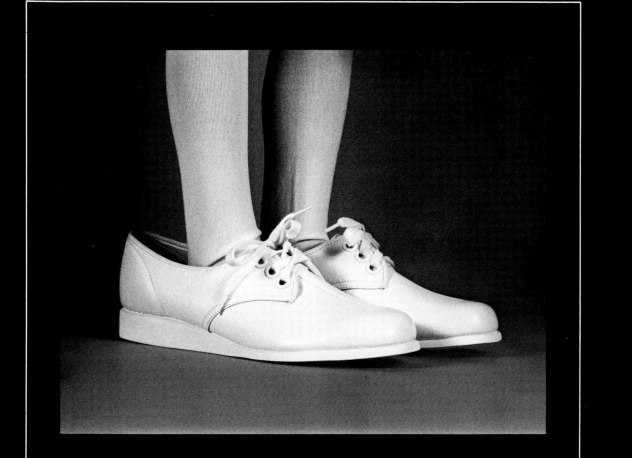

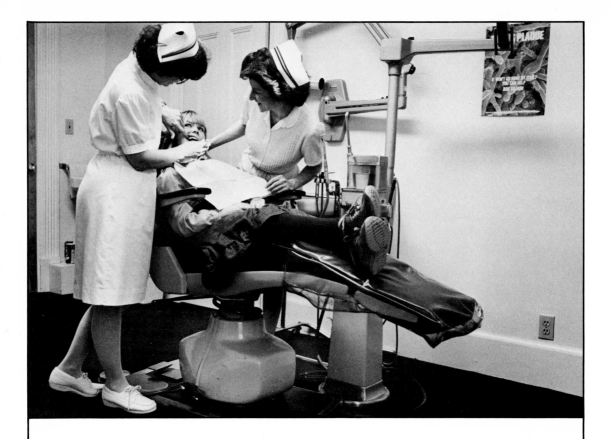

People who work in hospitals, nursing homes, and medical or dental offices often wear white shoes and white uniforms. Health care workers must be very clean to avoid spreading germs, and their white clothing quickly shows stains and dirt. Their shoes have thick rubber soles. That makes the shoes comfortable to stand in and quiet to walk in.

Why is this shoe made
of stretchy rubber?

This rubber shoe stretches to fit over a regular shoe. People wear overshoes to work, school, or play when the weather is wet. Overshoes can be easily slipped on to go outside, and they can be pulled off again inside a building. Many people carry overshoes in their pockets in case it rains or snows.

Long ago, towns in Europe had no sewers. Water had no place to drain, so the streets were often wet. People made their own work shoes, called clogs. They carved the soles out of wood and tacked on leather for the tops. Clogs kept the feet dry when people were outside. Today, many people wear clogs because they are comfortable.

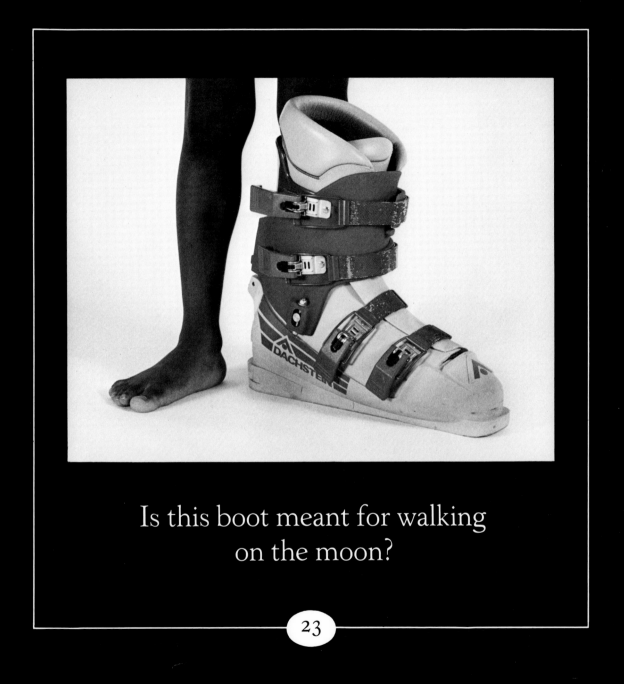

Is this boot meant for walking
on the moon?

No! This is a ski boot. When the four buckles are opened, a person's foot can easily slip into the boot. Ski boots are made of hard plastic to give support to a skier's ankles. The plastic won't crack or break even in the coldest weather. The little round knob on the side helps the skier tighten the boot so it fits perfectly over ski socks. When the boots are clamped onto the skis, it's time to go find the snow!

Why do these shoes
have flat toes?

These are toe shoes. They are worn by women ballet dancers who dance on their toes. The ribbons, elastic, and drawstring make the shoes fit perfectly and keep them in place on the dancer's feet. Inside the toes there are layers of cloth glued together and shaped into blocks. These blocks support the dancer's toes. Not all ballet dancers dance on their toes. Those who do must train for years to learn how.

Why does this sneaker
have knobs on the bottom?

This is a soccer shoe. The knobs are called spikes. These hard plastic spikes prevent players from slipping and falling on the soccer field. The spikes dig into the ground when a soccer player runs or stops quickly. The toe of the shoe is made of soft leather so the player can feel the ball as it is kicked. Feeling the ball lets a player kick it with better aim.

Who wears these
strange-looking shoes?

These are snowshoes. People wear them to walk on deep snow so their feet won't sink in. To move, you must glide over the snow with your feet wide apart. Walking this way, it is easy to fall! Snowshoes were first used in North America more than a thousand years ago. Early settlers bent branches into frames. Then they laced the frames with smaller branches or strips cut from animal skins.

Who wears boots with
such pointy toes?

Many horseback riders wear these western boots. The pointy toes easily slip into the stirrups, metal toeholds attached to straps on both sides of the saddle. With the feet in stirrups, a rider sits more securely in the saddle. Western boots are tall so the rider's ankles and lower legs don't rub against the saddle straps. These boots also protect the rider from scratchy bushes and rattlesnakes!

Who wears sneakers that lace
high on the ankle?

Basketball players wear these high-top sneakers. The players run, jump, twist, and turn on hard surfaces when they play. The high tops give support to the players' ankles. The rubber soles of the sneakers have ridges so the players can stop fast without slipping. Tiny holes in the sides of the sneakers let air inside to keep the players' feet cool.

When would you wear
such shiny shoes?

Many men wear these shiny black shoes made of patent leather on special occasions. Musicians and dancers who wear tuxedos when they perform often put on dressy shoes. There is something special about dressing up in a tuxedo and a pair of shiny, patent leather shoes. Some performers think they perform better when they are dressed in special clothing. What do you think?

Who wears shoes with tall,
thin heels?

Years ago in the courts of kings and queens, men as well as women wore shoes with high, shaped heels. Today many women wear these shoes for special dressy events. Such shoes make the wearer look taller. But shoes with high heels are hard to walk in for long distances—and very difficult to run in! Perhaps that is why people save these shoes for special occasions.

Who wears such long,
funny shoes?

Skippy the Clown wears these shoes. He likes to look silly to make people laugh. Skippy makes himself look funny by dressing in a colorful wig and costume. He covers his face with white makeup and sticks on a big red nose. Then he slips into his floppy clown shoes and ties the long laces. Flop flop flop, here comes Skippy!